PROJECT LUNA

An Agent Dancer Thriller

by Erik Parrent

D1304556

CHAPTER ONE

Another 1897...

All was well: the soft velvet of the chair, the warmth of the bourbon down the back of his throat, the thick haze of tobacco smoke in the air. He listened to the noises of the city, which were subdued at this time and place: the clip-clop of horse-drawn carriages, the distant cry of voices, the occasional rumble of a train. The noises inside the club were quieter still: conversation between gentlemen, the sound of the wait staff, the rustle of a newspaper or the clink of silverware. Philip Arthur Dancer enjoyed his well-earned leave.

Make no mistake, he enjoyed his work, but something about surviving a crashing train and a gunshot wound to the leg, not to mention that redhead, left even the strongest of men in need of some time to recuperate.

He looked around at the patrons of this, his favorite place in New York City, a club called the Silver Knife. Most of the patrons were businessmen, bankers, lawyers, men with soft hands and soft lives. Dancer's hands, indeed much of his body, were covered with scar tissue. He felt neither envy nor resentment when he observed the contrast with those around him; he had a job, he was good at it, and so he did it, allowing not just the people in the club but countless other citizens to lives safer and quieter than they might otherwise have been living.

He denied himself little when he wasn't doing that job: fine Kentucky bourbon, an excellent Cuban cigar, the thick, juicy steak he'd already had for dinner, perhaps the companionship of a beautiful woman. No one had assembled statistics yet on his line of work, but he'd be surprised if he had much of an old age to look forward to.

Dancer was an agent of the United States Secret Service.

He was the best they had.

And his leave was about to come to an unscheduled end.

Madeline Jarrell stepped out of the carriage in front of the brownstone. The brownstone resided in one of the more posh neighborhoods of New York, a place of quiet streets and old money. It stood far from the dirtier, noisier, rougher parts of the city, the parts that reminded her so much of the locale in which she had grown up.

The brownstone was five stories tall. The front door was made of a heavy wood, dark and polished, with a simple metallic nameplate that red "The Silver Knife."

"Wait here," she said to the driver of the carriage. She walked up the steps to the door, opened it, and entered.

A large man with short gray hair and a thick mustache stood behind a podium in the foyer of the building. He took one look at Madeline and said, "I'm sorry, young miss. This is a gentlemen-only establishment. I'll have to ask you to turn around and leave the way you came."

Madeline sighed deeply. She was in no mood for sexist garbage like this. As an agent of her country's secret service, she'd already saved the world too many times - this sorry excuse for a doorman included - to put up with it. She considered simply throwing him through a window, but decided that might have been a bit drastic. Instead, she handed him the card she'd been given.

The doorman looked at the card, his thick mustache drooping with his frown. He looked back up at Madeline. "You have my deepest apologies, young miss," he said. He handed the card back to her and gestured towards the stairs. "You may conduct your business at your leisure," he concluded.

It bothered Madeline that it was the name of a man on the card that gained her entry, but she didn't argue the point with the doorman. She nodded once to the man, smiling briefly and politely, and then made her way up the stairs.

She explored the club, looking for the gentleman she had been sent to find. She walked with deliberation through various rooms, some lined with wood paneling, some with rows of books, some with men playing billiards or cards. She passed men enjoying sumptuous meals, juicy steaks that made her stomach rumble. She studiously ignored the many indignant glances that came her way.

Madeline gave brief consideration to how useful an agent retrieved from such a place might actually be, an agent weighed down by rich food and drink and luxury, but discarded the thought.

Finally, just when she thought she might have been misinformed as to her quarry's location, she spotted the man she'd only seen in a single blurry photograph. He had risen from his chair and was walking across the room, stopping to speak with an attendant of some kind.

She judged he was in his mid-thirties, shorter than she had expected, about five feet and eight or nine inches tall. He wore an elegant black suit, likely expensive but with clean and simple lines. His brown hair was oiled back, and she was surprised to see a twinkle in his green eyes.

The twinkle bothered her. Someone in their line of work with a twinkle in his eye either didn't completely understand the situation or was, simply, crazy. She sighed again. Nothing for it at this point but to keep going.

Madeline approached the man. "Mr. Dancer?" she asked. He turned and looked at her. "Philip Arthur Dancer?" she continued.

"Yes. And you might be?" he asked.

"Jarrell. Madeline Jarrell."

Dancer looked at the girl. It was highly irregular to see a girl at all in the club, but she would've been unusual anywhere: hair dark as a raven's wing, skin the color of fresh cream, eyes the dark gray of a thundercloud. Her features were striking, lovely, even with the look of frustration. She wore a dress of dark red, with a black scarf and matching black boots. She was tall, and though she was clearly trying to hide it, she had the measured, economical, graceful movements of a dancer...

...or a warrior.

He offered his hand to her. "Ms. Jarrell," he said, "how may I help you?"

"I need you to come with me, sir," she replied. "You're needed."

"You may not have noticed, but I am on leave," he said. "The last time I checked, I was under no obligation to obey the orders of anyone at such a time."

"Just like a man to be so purposely obtuse," she said with a smirk. She produced the card. He looked at it for a moment like it might bite, then took it from her hand. He read the name on it and frowned.

"Bastard," he said. "He knows I'm on leave."

"He muttered something about how you were the best," she said. "I trust if that means anything to you, you'll be coming with me?"

"Naturally," he said with a smile.

It took but a few moments for Dancer to gather his coat, and he then followed Madeline down the stairs and out the front door. She was exquisite, and he liked that she apparently took guff from no one, but he knew better than to even think of someone in his line of work in anything remotely resembling a romantic fashion.

Jarrell led Dancer out the front door to the waiting carriage. They avoided small talk on the way down. She considered this a blessing.

She then considered the man himself for a moment. It's not that he wasn't handsome, or even appealing in his odd way, but her life was exceedingly complex for any sort of entanglements.

They entered the waiting carriage.

Dancer wasn't at all surprised whom he saw there. But he was angry.

CHAPTER TWO

"Bryant, you son of a whore," Dancer said, low and angry. "I'm on leave."

A casual observer would have seen only the subtle movements of a thick handlebar mustache, but to Dancer's eyes, the man in the carriage was smiling as broadly as a boy on his birthday.

Older than Dancer, by about ten years, he sat in the carriage, somehow managing to find shadow even in the daytime. He was thickly built, powerful but leaning to fat, with that thick mustache tinged with gray, as was his closely cropped gray hair.

His name was Reginald Bryant, and he was Dancer's master.

"Climb in, Philip, Ms. Jarrell," Bryant rumbled, in a low, deep voice not unlike the sound of a passing train. "I've got an assignment waiting."

No happier, Dancer entered the carriage, Jarrell close behind him. A word from Bryant to the driver, and they were moving through the streets.

"You had better have a damn good reason for this, Bryant," Dancer muttered darkly. "A damn. Good. Reason."

Bryant smiled again. "Aren't there people upon whom you wished revenge?" he asked.

Dancer grimaced. "Yes," he said. "But except for certain people in this carriage - by which I mean you - they're all dead now."

"Connor Dane," Bryant said.

"Is dead," Dancer answered.

"Is very much alive," Bryant corrected.

Dancer sat quietly for a long moment. "I've known you to be mistaken, Reginald," he finally said, "but never a liar."

"It's no lie, old friend," Bryant said. "We have reports of Conner Dane alive and well."

Dancer turned to stare out the window of the carriage. He was quiet and distant. Jarrell had the impression that in most ways that matter, he wasn't really in the carriage at all.

"He was my partner, and he betrayed me," Dancer finally said, in a voice barely above a whisper. "He sold me out. He sold our country out. And then he tried to kill me."

He turned to face Bryant, leaning forward in his seat. Jarrell wasn't sure Dancer was aware she was even there. "We fought on that airship," Dancer said, his voice growing tighter with anger. "I threw him out of the gondola with my own hands. I watched him fall until I couldn't see him anymore. There. Is. No. Way. He. Is. Alive."

"And yet," Bryant said, "our people in San Francisco have reported him attacking and damaging or destroying important scientific facilities in that city."

Dancer leaned back in his seat. "What sort of facilities?" he asked.

"Laboratories and facilities related to Project Luna," Bryant answered.

"Project Luna? What's that?" Dancer asked.

"It's a highly confidential program designed to place explorers on the moon," Bryant answered.

Jarrell remembered the first time Bryant had briefed her on Project Luna. She alternately laughed at the foolishness of such a project or swooned at its possibilities. She looked at Dancer and he looked as though he felt much the same way.

Bryant held up a hand. "Not joking, old friend. Not even a little," he said.

"How long," Dancer began slowly, "has this program been going on?" he asked.

"About four years now," Bryant answered, "although I'm told the scientific ground work was laid more than a decade ago."

"So you're asking me to postpone my leave so I can head west, find out whether or not my old partner is still alive and causing trouble, and keep a secret scientific endeavor from ending in catastrophe," Dancer said.

"That about sums it up," Bryant replied. "I know you've earned your rest this time. But given that it might actually be Mr. Dane, I thought you might want a piece of this one. For old times' sake, you know."

Dancer nodded. "You thought right," he said. "Will I be traveling alone?"

"No," Bryant answered. "Agent Jarrell here will be accompanying you. She's been fully briefed on Project Luna and is also exceedingly well trained and experienced in field work."

Dancer turned to Jarrell. He extended a hand. "He doesn't say those things lightly, Agent Jarrell, about anyone. I'm glad you're coming along."

She took his hand and gave it a firm shake. "Whatever's going on, we'll put a stop to it," she said. She turned to Bryant. "When do we leave?" she asked.

"As soon as possible," Bryant said. "I suspect Agent Dancer will have certain items he'll want to collect from his apartment. I'll have the carriage rider drop us there. Then you'll have a quick ride to Grand Central and be on your way."

CHAPTER THREE

Jarrell had no idea what to expect of Dancer's apartment. She supposed it might contain the excessively masculine - a lot of animal heads on walls, perhaps, or a pit in the floor with spikes.

She was surprised to find the top-floor dwelling to be elegant, sleek even, in shades of black, grey, and white, with sparse but comfortable furniture, and the occasional tasteful work of art on the wall. One could see a fine stretch of the city through the large windows. The place smelled of tobacco and expensive cologne, but not overpoweringly so.

Jarrell occupied a small sofa in the great room. On a nearby table was a suitcase of polished dark brown leather, into which Dancer was packing various items.

Dancer emerged from his bedroom with a stack of neatly folded shirts. He placed them in the suitcase. He asked Jarrell, "So, tell me about Project Luna."

He continued back and forth, packing, as Jarrell explained the project to him.

"It began when a Lieutenant Wells, a cavalry officer with scientific leanings, discovered an exotic mineral in the Arizona territory," she began. "It was exceedingly light and strong, by several factors better than the finest steel. That fact alone would have rendered it remarkable. But Wells then discovered quite by accident that the mineral manifests some kind of energy field that, when purified, allows it to defy gravity."

Dancer continued to pack. She wasn't entirely sure he believed any of this. "What did he call it?" Dancer asked.

"Wellsite," she answered.

He stopped dead in his tracks. "You must be joking," he said.

"Not even a little," she answered. After a long moment, they resumed.

"So, naturally, he decides to go to the moon," Dancer said.

Jarrell shook her head. "Of course not. He conceived, perhaps, of advanced attack airships, or something similar. He suggested nothing so extravagant as traveling to the moon, in part because he lacks imagination, in part because the mineral is quite rare, and in part because it generates on its own no propulsion."

Dancer noted as he neatly stowed a pearl-colored waistcoat in his case. "So where did that part of the equation come from?" he asked.

"A scientist, a man named James Verne, who works for a concern named Vatine Metallique," Jarrell said. "Wells decided to explore various possibilities for the mineral. Verne had the vision necessary for Project Luna. He took it to his employer, the owner and operator of Vatine Metallique, Veronique Vatine. She successfully persuaded the army that the project was worth pursuing and they have been working in secret, and in tandem, for several years now."

"Several years?" Dancer asked. "So is the project close to fruition?"

"Very," Jarrell answered. "The testing phase is completed. Launch of a vehicle capable of visiting the moon and returning is only weeks away. So, you understand why Mr. Dane's insistence on not being dead is quite troublesome."

"It would be," Dancer said, as he closed and locked his suitcase. "That should do it," he said with satisfaction. "Have you any baggage, Miss Jarrell?" he asked.

"Mine is already aboard our airship," she answered primly. "I trust you have everything you need?"

"Almost," he said. "We have one stop we need to make before departing."

She looked at his massive suitcase. "I can't imagine what else you would need," she said.

"I usually can't, either," he said with a smile. "Thankfully, I have a fellow who's very good at imagining it for me."

They stepped from the carriage onto a sooty, noisy street. Jarrell looked at the storefront before them and was singularly unimpressed.

She looked at Dancer. He wore the expression of a child preparing to storm a candy store.

"Herr Goff is very good at what he does," Dancer said. "I think you'll be pleased."

"You've been very circumspect about precisely what it is that he does, Mr. Dancer. Would you care to elaborate while you still have time?" Jarrell asked.

Dancer looked at her with a gleam of anticipation in his eyes. "He has a unique ability to construct equipment for the members of our curious profession," he said.

"Oh," Jarrell said. "We're going to a toy store."

A bell jingled as Dancer opened the door, graciously allowing Jarrell to enter first. The store was quite clean and brightly lit, especially compared to the dirty street outside, but far from neat or orderly. Clutter occupied every available inch of every available surface. She thought the disarray might give her hives and tried desperately to avoid touching anything.

She observed Dancer as he, to the contrary, examined each individual item with undeniable glee: a wrist sheath for a set of gleaming silver knives, a vest woven from metallic fibers, a tiny pistol hidden within an umbrella's handle.

"Herr Goff?" he called. "Herr Goff, it's Philip Dancer."

A man appeared from the array of gadgets. He was tall, with gold-rimmed glasses and curly blonde hair, and a midsection the large size of which was ill hidden by a white lab coat and a generous tool belt.

"Mr. Dancer!" he said with a Germanic lilt in his voice. "How pleasant to see you!"

16

"And very pleasant to see you as well, Herr Goff," Dancer replied. "My companion and I are scheduled to depart on a journey within the hour, and as you're aware I always make your shop my last stop on the way out of town."

Goff smiled broadly. "And may I inquire," he said, "where your journey may take you?"

Jarrell was about to object to important operational information being made public to a mad tinkerer, but Dancer spoke before she could stop him. "Out west," Dancer replied. "Possibly near water."

She found that vague enough to allow the conversation to continue.

Goff considered for a moment. "You would be traveling by airship, Mein Herr? So you would need to pack light, no?"

"That would be convenient, yes," Dancer answered.

Jarrell had to expend effort to keep from snorting with laughter as she thought about the enormous suitcase Dancer had packed.

"I have just the thing," Goff said. To Jarrell's amazement he walked amongst the clutter and picked from it a single box, as if he knew precisely where each bit of equipment was to be found. The box was only a few inches across, and covered in deep blue velvet. He handed it to Dancer, who opened it, and then smiled like a little boy on Christmas morning.

"Cartridges," he said, with a proud smile. "Several of them, all in the precise caliber of your preferred pistol, if I'm not mistaken. And each one capable of an entirely different effect."

Dancer closed the case and shook Goff's hand. "Thank you for your usual sterling work, Herr Goff," he said.

"The usual financial arrangements?" Goff asked.

"Certainly. Send the bill to Mr. Bryant, per the usual," Dancer said. "It's on the company tab, Ms. Jarrell. See anything you like?" he asked.

She shook her head. "No. I'm sure your work is exemplary, Mr. Goff, but I have my preferred equipment already secured aboard our transportation."

Goff nodded. "I understand. But I do hope you'll visit my shop again sometime, and give me a chance to devise some armaments perfect for you?"

"Certainly," she replied politely.

"One more thing, Mr. Dancer," Goff asked. "Could I convince you to try out my wingpak?"

Dancer laughed. "Herr Goff, I trust you with my life, but you'll have to find someone braver than I to sample that contraption," he said.

"Wingpak?" Jarrell asked.

"Yes," Dancer went on. "A thing of wood and brass similar to a daVinci drawing. It's supposed to let a man fly under his own power from a great height. Herr Goff keeps attempting to sell me one, but my good sense keeps winning out and I keep refusing."

Jarrell looked at Goff. "I may try that someday, Herr Goff," she said, turning to face Dancer. "Just to see the look on Dancer's face when I fly."

Goff laughed heartily as Dancer and Jarell left his store.

CHAPTER FOUR

The carriage dropped Dancer and Jarrell off at Grand Central Station, but the great railroad terminal was not their final destination. They quickly found a nearby marble-and-glass building with the name McNeely Air Transit.

A McNeely porter, in his distinct, crisp blue and gold uniform, gathered their bags, and in moments they were inside the building and onto a lift platform, where they joined a number of finely dressed passengers. The lift jerked, and with a hiss of steam began to move upwards.

Soon they were on top of the building, at a different sort of terminal altogether, one for the airships of McNeely Air. Indeed, one of the great vessels waited for them, the *Alexis Bouvard*. It loomed above them, the distinct blue and gold of McNeely Air extending to the fittings of the craft.

Dancer, Jarrell, and the other passengers walked up a secure gangplank to the gondola. They were welcomed aboard by the crew, and then walked aft through the dining compartment and up into the ship's passenger space.

As soon as the passengers and crew were secure, the crew cast off the ship's moorings. The engines started with a deep rumble, and they were in the air and heading west.

The *Alexis Bouvard* rose gracefully into the air. Unknown to any of her passengers, a small man in a gray suit observed her from a nearby building.

The man entered a stairwell, unhurried, and took those stairs to the street several stories below. He walked to the nearest Western Union he could find, entered, and sent a telegram.

It contained four words: Dancer, Jarrell, *Alexis Bouvard*.

And it was addressed only to "Mr. Jones."

Dancer adored airship travel, in part because it was faster than anything over land, including rail, in part because the vistas from such great heights gave him perspective, but mostly because it was quiet.

He sat in his exceptionally comfortable leather chair in the dining compartment of the *Alexis Bouvard*, sipping his drink. The bourbon was from Kentucky, of course, and quite good. But all he could hear was the clink of silverware on china, a murmur of low conversation, and the distant thrumming of the airship's great engines.

A rustle of fabric behind him heralded the approach of Madeline Jarrell. She sat down across from him and gestured towards a waiter. "Thank you for waiting to order," she said.

"As a gentleman would," he responded.

The waiter arrived. Jarrell ordered hot, sweet coffee, and then she and Dancer made their meal choices. The waiter departed.

"We've been in the air a while now," she began. "You've kept to yourself, which is fine, but I think I'm owed a degree of...historical information, let's say."

Dancer nodded. "You mean Connor Dane," he said.

She nodded.

Dancer took another sip of his drink.

"You're right, of course," he said.

He steadied himself.

"We met as very young men, in school in upstate New York," Dancer said. "We became friends immediately. We had a great deal in common, from our families to a great many basic ideas about the world, as well as our dreams."

The waiter returned with a steaming mug of coffee for Jarrell. "What were those dreams?" she asked, before sampling her drink.

"We had the idea that we'd like to make the world a better place," he answered. "Neither of our families was wealthy, but we also lacked for little, and their seemed to be a great deal of suffering we wanted to alleviate if we could. And then Reginald Bryant found us, and turned us into the agents, the soldiers, the...weapons his service needed. And that was well with us. It was good work and it needed doing."

Dancer turned and looked out the window. Jarrell saw something in his eyes she couldn't place, something she hadn't seen there before. Was he...haunted? What on earth could this man be haunted by? she thought.

He took a deep breath and went on. "I've lost track of everywhere we went and everything we did. He was my brother, and I was his. But somewhere along the line...Something changed.

"I couldn't tell you when. And so help me, I don't understand why. But the look in his eyes changed. He was cruel when he didn't have to be. He took risks he didn't need to take. He started to keep secrets."

Jarrell snorted. "Are you describing your ex-partner or an ex-wife?" she said.

Dancer was not amused. "And then on our last mission, mere months ago, he tried to kill me. He stuck a knife in me and tried to push me off an airship over Colorado," he told her.

Jarrell was quiet as she listened.

"We fought and I pushed him off instead. I watched him fall, but he disappeared into the clouds and I blacked out from blood loss.

"I found a bag of money - a lot of money - in his quarters. I don't know who it was from or what duties he was expected to perform for it, save that it meant one thing: he betrayed me, he betrayed his service and he betrayed his country," he finished.

The sumptuous meal finally came, and they ate and savored it in silence. Jarrell finally spoke first. "I'm sorry," she said.

"I appreciate the sentiment, but don't bother saying it again. We work in a hard line, and there's nothing for it but to soldier on," he said. "Besides, we have a new problem, I think."

"What's that?" she said.

"Listen," he said.

She did. Her expression told him she'd heard the same thing.

"Travel by airship is quiet," Dancer began. "Not the ships themselves, of course, but because of the rarefied atmosphere in which they operate. One advantage of that is you can hear another one coming."

CHAPTER FIVE

Dancer and Jarrell hurried to a nearby window. They looked out at the endless blue sky for the approaching airship.

Jarrell saw it first. "There," she said, pointing to a swiftly-moving shape of mottled blue and gray.

Dancer realized the implications. "That ship is camouflaged," he said. "That pattern of gray and blue is supposed to render a ship difficult to spot until it's too late for the attacker to run."

Jarrell listened to the sounds of their own ship. "It sounds like the captain is ordering the engines to higher speeds."

"No doubt," Dancer said. "But it's already too late. They'll be on us in minutes."

Dancer turned to Jarrell. "The last time I got into a battle on an airship, I was betrayed by my partner and almost died," he said. "I trust you have some ideas about how this may go better for us?"

Jarrell thought for a moment. "They're camouflaged," she said. "They were on us before we even knew they were coming. The could already have destroyed us if they wanted."

Dancer picked up the thread of her thought. "Which means they intend to board us. Which means, whatever their goal...someone needs to be sure of something," he said.

"Which gives us the advantage," she said. "We don't have to be as careful as they do."

They looked back out the windows. The second airship was approaching, at a higher altitude. They could now clearly make out the gondola of the other craft. A hatch in the side slipped open. Soon, three individuals in tight-fitting gray flight gear emerged, perched on the edge of the hatch.

The first out spread his arms, revealing a wrist-to-ankle gliding array on both sides of his body. He threw himself into space from the safety of the hatchway, catching the winds in his glider suit, and soared like a bird of prey directly at Dancer and Jarrell's transport.

The first attacker passed out of Dancer's sight. Barely an instant later, Dancer heard a thump that shook the gondola, followed by the sound of glass shattering.

The second attacker leapt into the sky after the first, gliding down in much the same way, followed swiftly by the third. The attacking ship then began to move downwards.

"They intend to leave the same way," Jarrell said. "They intend to glide down to the mother ship."

"People intend all kinds of things that are never going to happen," Dancer said. "Don't you agree?"

Jarrell smiled, the smile of a wolf, the smile of a warrior. Dancer looked his new partner in the eyes. What he saw would have scared another man, more than a little. He was glad she was on the same side as he.

Somewhere in the ship, Dancer heard a cry of fear. He turned to Jarrell. She nodded to him, and without a word they raced towards the sounds of trouble.

The observation deck was a hell in the skies.

The three attackers in gray had smashed in through the glass of the compartment. Wind from the high altitudes roared through the chamber, making it impossible to hear. An innocent observer, a well-dressed older man, hung desperately from the ship. He was clinging to a broken window frame when Dancer and Jarrell hurtled into the room.

At that moment, the older man's grip failed, and he plunged from the frame to his doom.

His terrified cry cut through the noise of the wind. That scream, like so many before, would haunt Dancer.

And it would fuel him, as well - he would use the memory to stoke his fury like an engine of hate, to sharpen his senses, to make each blow in the coming battle as precise as possible.

The three attackers were already moving towards Dancer and Jarrell. Two of them broke off and headed towards Jarrell. The other paused a moment, sized up Dancer, and moved in.

Dancer sized the man up. He was tall and lean. His leather flight suit looked to be sturdy. His glider array was already retracted into some sort of sheath. He wore a padded gray helmet with a set of heavy goggles and a scarf covering his mouth.

He threw a punch. Dancer blocked it, easily, as well as the next two. Then a flurry of blows in a fighting style Dancer didn't recognize each found their mark, and Dancer staggered to his knees.

Jarrell was faring better. Dancer could pay little attention to her battle, but out of the corner of his eye he saw her move like a prima ballerina, swooping and diving, a blur as she dodged punch after kick after punch.

He didn't know what her endgame was. He didn't have time to think about it. His opponent struck brutally, then thrust his knee at Dancer's jaw.

Somehow Dancer found the strength to dodge, but the knee still connected, somewhere around his right shoulder. Dancer rose, inelegant but powerful, and slammed into the man, and together they crashed into the bulkhead.

The man's fists sought Dancer's ribs, but he couldn't find the leverage he needed to make the blows count. Dancer struggled to inflict damage, but the man's flight suit prevented it.

The flight suit -

Dancer grabbed along the man's sides. He found what he sought: the glider array. Dancer grabbed the faux wings and tore for all he was worth.

Hunks of fabric and metal came out in Dancer's hands. Dancer heard the man's screams over the sound of the wind.

Try to get away without your wings, Dancer thought, smiling grimly.

The smile set the attacker off. He lunged at Dancer, fury in his eyes, all thought of careful attack now gone as his chances of escape were rendered moot.

Dancer blocked the man's attacks, easily. He moved around the cabin, the flight-suited man following him, attacking in blind rage.

He thought he heard Jarrell, just for a moment, but couldn't tell for sure over the wind and the sounds of combat.

Finally, the man took a chance on a roundhouse punch at Dancer -

Dancer ducked, the attacker's momentum carrying him forward -

Dancer stood, flipping the attacker over and out the shattered window.

Dancer collapsed to the floor of the observation deck, breath coming in hot ragged gasps.

He saw Jarrell.

Her dark hair swirled in disarray around her head. Her dress was torn and stained - hopefully with someone else's blood.

And she was alone, her attackers dispatched.

"I thought I told you to save one for questioning!" she shouted.

Dancer could do little but shrug.

CHAPTER SIX

The red brick house stood in a run-down section of San Francisco. It was nondescript, almost totally anonymous.

Conner Dane thought this made it an excellent place to meet.

It was one of several safe houses he maintained on his own dime, privately, outside anyone's knowledge. He would abandon it after this meeting, its usefulness finished to him.

Dane waited in what was once an elegant dining room, a simple table with a pair of chairs now the only furnishings. The front door opened and closed, and Dane heard the floorboards creak as his visitor approached.

Dane judged that the man was close to fifty years of age, and dressed entirely in black, from his boots to his hat to the bag he carried. His dark blonde hair was pulled back in a queue that hung down his back.

"A bit theatrical, aren't we?" the man asked in an accent Dane placed as London.

"Mr. Jones," Dane began, "please have a seat." Dane knew the name was an alias, but didn't care.

Dane didn't rise but let Jones pull out his own chair and have a seat. His money was good. That didn't make Dane his butler.

"I require a progress report," Jones began.

"The harassment of Project Luna continues," Dane said. "I have caused substantial losses of materiel. Key personnel have left the project."

"But the launch is still on schedule," Jones said.

"It is," Dane said.

"It must be halted," Jones continued. "The Americans must not be allowed to succeed. The men for whom I work could not countenance such an insult to their national pride."

Dane actually couldn't care less who those men were. As long as the money was good, he would do whatever job he had to.

Dane considered for a moment. "I told you doing that would be difficult for one man," he said. "There is a considerable military presence around the project."

"And there will soon be secret service agents assigned to the project, as well," Jones said.

This gave Dane a start, but he managed not to show it. "Do you know whom?" he asked casually.

"Their names are Dancer and Jarrell," Jones said.

Dane's face betrayed nothing, but he knew if Dancer were on his way...

Well. Best to wrap this affair up as quickly as possible. Dancer occasionally took things somewhat personally.

"If you need the Project destroyed, I'll need to hire some men. And that will mean money," Dane said.

"That's what the bag is for," Jones said.

Jones rose from his seat, leaving the bag. He made for the front door. "Do not fail us," Jones said. "Or there are men who will come for you."

The door slammed shut. Dane was unconcerned about the threat. There was no one in the world Jones could hire he would be afraid of.

No. The one man of any concern to Dane... was already on his way.

CHAPTER SEVEN

Jarrell thought she could smell a faint hint of salt air as she stood on the streets of San Francisco.

The streetcar pulled away, rattling as it went. She and Dancer had just disembarked from the car, and stood in front of the destination they had crossed America to reach: the headquarters of Vatine Metallique

Jarrell stared up at the building. It was not the tallest around, but it was surely the most modern, brass and steel gleaming in the morning sunlight.

Dancer turned to her. "They're expecting us," he said.

"Let's not disappoint them," Jarrell said, and they entered the building.

The night before, after hours in the restaurant of their hotel, Jarrell briefed Dancer on Vatine Metallique, the clatter of wait staff in the background.

Jarrell took a drink of coffee. "It's a construction firm specializing in airships," she began. "Founded in France in 1876 by Jacques Vatine. Had a few rough years before finding its stride. Its airships are considered the standard by which others are measured.

"Jacques met Veronique in 1882. She studied engineering at a prestigious Belgian college, the first woman to do so there," Jarrell said. Dancer could detect the admiration in her voice.

"Their attraction was instant and mutual. Jacques married Veronique in 1885. It was a lavish ceremony by all accounts. Veronique became part of the business and their fortunes rose even higher," Jarrell continued.

Dancer picked at the remains of his meal, and took a sip of coffee. "How did they come to the U.S.?" he asked.

Jarrell paused. "It was Veronique's idea," she said. "It was a simple matter of ambition. They had conquered the market in Europe. Why not conquer the market in America as well?

"They established offices in San Francisco. Things began well. Then Jacques was killed in an accident testing a new model of airship," Jarrell said.

"How did she take it?" Dancer asked.

"Badly," Jarrell answered. "Their love was genuine and deep. She left the running of the firm to trusted advisors and locked herself away in the top floor living quarters of their San Francisco HQ.

"It's possible she would have stayed there, maybe even wasting away until death, had not Project Luna captured her imagination," she said.

"Why that? What was it?" Dancer asked.

Jarrell leaned back, clearing considering her words. "I think it was the challenge," she said. "Remember, she's an engineer first, as was poor Jacques. Why, the very idea! A ship to the moon? It's outlandish, ridiculous. But imagine it - being the one who led mankind to another world. The possibility would be...irresistible."

Dancer sipped his coffee again. "Then let's make sure her ambition is thwarted no longer," he said.

Jarrell smiled. They each lifted their cups and clinked them together.

Two large men in nondescript suits met Dancer and Jarrell in the lobby of the building. One of them spoke. "Come with us," he said, his voice rumbling and deep.

Dancer nodded once, and they followed the men to the glass-and-brass lift. It sped quickly to the top floor, and Dancer and Jarrell exited along with the two guards.

Dancer had expected a certain amount of luxury in Vatine's private quarters, and he was not disappointed. The top floor of the building was one large open space, and he could see a formal dining table, an elaborate kitchen, a spacious formal sitting area, and an area contained within sheer hanging silks that he assumed was Vatine's bedchamber.

What he didn't expect was the clutter. Blueprints. Slide rules. Bits of machines, whether functional or not he couldn't tell. Papers. Pencils. Pens. Pieces of canvas. Clothes scattered all over because their owner could not be troubled to put them away. Books on engineering, books on physics, books on chemistry, novels, books of poetry. Dirty dishes. Empty glasses.

"Perhaps she needs to hire a maid," Dancer said.

"I would never," said Veronique Vatine.

Dancer saw her emerge from behind a chalkboard. His breath immediately caught in his throat.

She was a bit over five feet tall. Her blonde hair swirled around her head, pencils sticking from it, fastened loosely with a dark blue ribbon. Her fair skin was flawless and her crystalline blue eyes crackled with an intelligence and energy Dancer had never seen before. The loose coverall she wore was smeared with dark splotches of ink or oil or grease, Dancer wasn't sure.

"You see, I have a system," Vatine continued. "I know where every blueprint, pen, pencil, dish and undergarment is. A maid would only disrupt things."

Her French accent was light but unmistakable. Dancer held out his hand.

"Dancer," he said. "Philip Arthur Dancer. At your service."

Madeline stepped up beside Dancer. "Madeline Jarrell," she said. "We're here to help."

Vatine looked them both up and down. "So I have been told," she said. "Come. Sit."

The guards left. Vatine led Dancer and Jarrell to the sitting area. She moved a large pile of schematics from a couch to the floor and gestured for her guests to sit, which they did.

Vatine perched on the edge of a magnificently overstuffed chair and proceeded to curl up in it like a cat.

"I have lost facilities," she began. "I have lost materiel. And most troubling, most tragic, I have lost good people. I seek to do something revolutionary, remarkable, something to change the arc of the human story, and have been met with violence and destruction for so doing."

"That's what we are here to investigate and to stop," Dancer said. "What can you tell us about the attacks on your facilities?"

Vatine reached out to a nearby table and grabbed a thick folder. She tossed it to Jarrell, who caught it easily.

"It's all there," she said. "Every clue we have, every loss."

Jarrell undid the band on the folder and opened it. On top of the stack of documents was a photograph of a man.

"We were able to salvage that photograph from the most recent attack," Vatine said. "We were testing cameras for the ship and the one that took that photograph survived."

Jarrell looked at the photo and handed it to Dancer.

Jarrell would swear she could feel the room turn colder.

"It's not possible," he whispered.

The photo was of a man, tall, rugged, with a scar over one eye, and a handsome face that bent towards cruelty.

Jarrell put her hand on Dancer's forearm.

"It's Dane," he said. "It's Connor Dane."

Dancer turned to Vatine. "I know who this man is," he said. "And I swear to you, he will meet his end at my hand."

CHAPTER EIGHT

The sunset provided a warm scarlet glow to an otherwise cold scene of destruction.

The building had been a place of science and innovation, a Vatine Metallique facility devoted to systems design for Project Luna.

Now it was shattered. Two of the outside walls were twisted, open to the sky, blasted outwards by a saboteur's bomb. Fire had scorched the whole of the building. The explosion had reduced the work done by the scientists and engineers on staff to the rubble that crunched beneath Dancer's boots.

Dancer observed the wreckage. He could feel his face getting hotter as he got angrier. He glanced at Jarrell. He could tell by the look on her face that she shared his anger.

Dancer then looked to Veronique. She looked around her, seeing the place where her friends had died and her dreams had been assaulted. Dancer could see the tears forming around her eyes and practically feel the resolve she spent in holding them back.

It was the third such place that they had visited that day. Poison gas had felled the personnel in the first facility. An appalling chemical fire had incinerated the second facility.

"I will shed no more tears," Veronique said. Dancer wasn't sure if it was intended for him and Jarrell or more for herself. "I shall devote the energy elsewhere."

Veronique turned to him. "We have surveyed the sight of your old friend's handiwork, Mr. Dancer," she said. "I do sincerely hope that these little excursions have taught you something of value."

Dancer took a moment to consider. Jarrell looked to him as well, an eyebrow raised as if to say it was time to produce some kind of result.

"I think," Dancer said, "that despite being dead, he hasn't lost a step."

On the last word, Dancer whirled. As part of the same smooth motion, he pulled his gun from its shoulder holster.

In that moment Jarrell and Veronique saw what had spurred Dancer to action: a man, clad in black, had appeared as if from nowhere, also brandishing a gun. He was attempting to bring it to bear as Dancer took aim and fired a single round.

The attacker cried out once, spun and fell.

Then something strange happened. Veronique, Jarrell, and Dancer felt a blast of cold air on their faces. They approached their fallen foe.

He was frozen in place, his face a mask of gruesome death.

Veronique was amazed. "How did you accomplish such a thing?" she asked, amazement in her voice.

"I am acquainted with an engineer in New York. One who specializes in arms and equipment for my peculiar profession," he said. "Before we departed he prepared me with an array of six bullets, each designed for a different effect."

"You might have used another one," Jarrell said. "We could have questioned him had he remained alive."

"There's nothing else he could have told us that his presence doesn't already confirm," Dancer said. "The attack itself confirms Dane is still in the city and still actively pursuing his campaign. Bane is too good at his work to have left any connection to this man we could use to find him."

He turned to Veronique. "Do you know this man?" he asked.

"No," she replied simply.

"Then we are done with him," Dancer replied.

"So," Veronique said, "have our travels this day told you anything useful? Or have I endured this grief again for nothing?"

Dancer took her hand. "On the contrary," he said. "He's told me a great deal. Each of the attacks we have studied today has been carried out with skills Bane does not possess."

"But we have his photograph," Veronique said.

"Indeed," said Jarrell, realization spreading across her face. "Which means he sought to conceal his identity by having others do his blood work for him."

"Exactly," said Dancer. "Tell me, Veronique - where do you think one would go in San Francisco to hire a mercenary?"

CHAPTER NINE

Veronique smiled for the first time that day. "My husband had need of extra security, some years back," she said. "He consulted with other men of his standing and they provided him with a name and a place. His contact was to be found at a tavern, an extremely disreputable establishment called the Bronze Lantern."

Dancer nodded. "What did he tell you about it?"

"Very little," she said. "He sought to protect me from some of the things he had to do. But that is where he found a contact and men to hire."

"I don't suppose he told you the name of his contact?" Jarrell asked.

"No," Veronique said. "He said I was better off not knowing. But he did say that she was quite unmistakable."

The doors swung open. The bar on the other side reeked of sweat and alcohol. Jarrell also detected the faint bouquet of desperation.

She and Dancer entered. Dimly lit in the first place, she had to squint to see through the thick haze of smoke.

"Who do you suppose we're looking for? Jarrell asked.

"No way to know," Dancer asked. "All we can do is stay alert to our surroundings and be prepared to act."

They walked through the Bronze Lantern. It teemed with customers, some loud and raucous, having a rousing good time, and some silent, staring into a drink as though to forget God knew what.

Each customer looked dangerous. Each had the potential to wield the blade that killed them.

They found an unoccupied table. A waiter soon tended to them. Assuming the finer vintages were not available, Dancer and Jarrell each ordered a beer.

Their drinks were soon in their hands. A sip was all either required to discover that people did not patronize the Bronze Lantern for its fine drinks.

Dancer's face wrinkled in disgust he could not hide.

"Not your club, is it?" Jarrell asked.

"I'd say we are very far, in every possible sense, from my club," Dancer asked.

They surveyed the room. They studied every face.

Finally Dancer saw her.

The late Mr. Vatine was right - she was quite unmistakable.

For one thing, despite the foamy mug in front of her, she appeared quite sober.

She sat alone in her booth. She wore a man's suit, obviously both expensive and expensively tailored. Her sleek silver hair was pulled back in a long braid. Dancer estimated she was in her mid to late sixties. Where age sometimes dimmed physical beauty in both men and women, this had not happened to her - she was striking.

But more than that, her eyes were piercing. They scanned the room with a terrifying focus.

And they locked onto Dancer's.

He smiled. "What's happening?" Jarrell asked.

"It's showtime," he said. "Follow my lead and be prepared for anything."

Dancer rose from the table. Jarrell followed. Soon they were sitting across from the woman.

"I see you left your drinks," she said.

They each nodded.

"Meaning of course that you were not here to drink in the first place," she said.

"Calling them drinks might be an insult to warm piss," Dancer said.

The woman smiled. "I am the Broker," she said. "Judging by your dress, your lives seem significantly less...marginal than most of the men I see here. What do you seek?"

Dancer and Jarrell traded a look. Jarrell took the lead.

"We're new in town," she said. "And we're seeking employment. We have, as they say, specialized skills. We excel at removing men from this mortal coil."

The Broker nodded. "Your names?"

Dancer spoke first. "Paris," he said.

Jarrell followed. "London," she said.

The Broker nodded. "I see. You like your anonymity. Very well."

She took a blank card from inside her jacket, followed by a pencil. She wrote an address and a time on it and passed the card to Dancer.

"There's a man securing talent such as yourselves," the Broker said. "If you were known to me, I could procure more lucrative assignments for you. As it is... We will begin here. Do not be late."

Dancer stuck the card in his jacket. "You won't regret this."

The Broker gave him a hard look. "See that I don't."

Dancer and Jarrell rose and left the bar.

A moment passed. Then two.

Finally Conner Dane sat down at the booth with the Broker.

"In town less than a day," the Broker said. "And already he's deduced how to find you, Mr. Dane."

"He's quite good, you know," Dane said. "If he were to strike out on his own he'd make a fortune in short order. Too much of a conscience for that, though. Still believes in things like honor and duty."

"What do you plan to do?" the Broker asked. "I would rather not have my enterprise ended by complications caused by you."

"Persuade him to change his mind," Dane said. "Or end him."

CHAPTER TEN

It was clear to Dancer, even in these hours before dawn, that the neighborhood had seen better days. He wondered what had caused the decline. Then he found their destination and had time to wonder no more.

The red brick house was fairly nondescript. He checked the address the Broker had written on the card and saw that they had found the correct place.

He turned to Jarrell. He almost wondered aloud, *Is he here? Will I find Connor Dane in this house?*

The way she returned his look told him that he didn't have to ask. She knew what he was thinking.

Without a word, they walked across the weed-strewn yard. They made a quick circle of the house, finding no one and nothing to cause suspicion. Returning to the front, they knocked on the door.

A year later, the door opened.

Connor Dane stood before them.

He smiled broadly. "Phil!" he said. "Why don't you and your friend here come on in!"

Dancer's face and body betrayed not even the least emotion as he entered the house. Jarrell did likewise behind him.

A single light burned in the dining room. A plate of bread and fruit and cheese sat on the table there, with mugs of what looked like Guinness beside it.

"A little light food," Dane said. "I know you've had a long journey to get here."

Jarrell and Dancer looked warily at the spread before them. Dane figured out what bothered them.

"It's good," he said. "No poisons or toxins, I promise. This is just to talk."

"Why shouldn't I just shoot you now?" Dancer asked.

"Curiosity," Dane answered. "You just have to know why."

Dancer, frustrated, sat at the table. He placed his hand in his coat pocket. "You're right, of course," he said.

Jarrell did not sit, but did take a piece of cheese to nibble on.

"And who are you?" Dane asked.

"Jarrell," she said. "Bryant sends his regards, by the way."

Dane smiled. "Yes, I'm sure he does," he said.

"Why, Connor?" Dancer asked.

"You still get right to the point, don't you?" Dane asked. "Fine. Money, mostly."

Jarrell shook her head. "What?" she asked. "You betrayed him for money?"

"Of course," Dane said. "What else is there?"

Dancer took a drink of the dark Guinness on the table. "I thought we believed in something," he said.

"You believed in something," Dane answered.

The two men looked at each other.

"You were my friend, Phil," Dane said. "I followed you because of that. *You* were the idealist. *You* had honor. *You* had hope. I never believed in much of anything. And then after a while the scar tissue started to add up, and not much else did."

Jarrell circled them as they talked.

"Our work paid well," Dancer said.

"Not enough," Dane said, anger creeping into his voice for the first time. "I was beaten, stabbed, shot, feared for my life over and over as one madman after another threatened everything. And I was expected to just handle it."

"You could have told me," Dancer said, taking a drink.

Dane looked away. "It was easier to just stab you," he said.

"I saw you fall from that airship," Dancer said. "I thought you were dead."

Dane grinned. "I have Herr Goff to thank for that," he said.

Dancer's face turned pale. "The wingpak," he said.

"Just so," Dane said.

Jarrell interrupted. "Money," she said. "Is that why you have attacked Vatine Metallique?"

"Of course," he said. "I could care less what they do. But I am being paid well."

"By whom?" Dancer asked.

"Ah, ah," Dane said. "No far asking. And anyway, it doesn't matter. I don't know who it is. The money comes via courier or wire transfer and it's good."

Dane looked at them. "You could always join me," he said.

Dancer almost smiled. "I appreciate the invitation," he said. "But no."

"Then there's only one way this job ends, for either of us," Dane said.

"I know," Dancer said. "And this time I'll be sure."

"As will I," Dane said.

In a flash Dane had produced a gun, a revolver in his right hand. As time slowed down Jarrell could see his finger tighten on the trigger.

A gunshot smashed the silence of the room.

A cloud of dark gray smoke swirled around them.

Dane cried out in anger and began firing.

Jarrell felt a hand grab hers and pull her roughly. She trusted it was Dancer and followed it.

A moment later they were crashing out of the smoke and through a doorway into the backyard. In the dim light of the quickening dawn she saw it was Dancer indeed who had her. They raced through the alleys and yards of the neighborhood until they were quite sure that they had eluded Dane.

They were each breathing heavy.

"Gun in your pocket, I suppose?" Jarrell asked.

"Smoke cartridge," Dancer replied.

"Hell of an engineer, that Goff," she said.

CHAPTER ELEVEN

Dancer and Jarrell returned to their rooms for much needed rest. Dancer, after sleep, a shower, and a shave, cabled Bryant with the results of their investigation. He then joined Jarrell in her room. She also had had a chance for sleep and a shower and seemed as refreshed as Dancer.

"You could have shot him," she said.

"Not really," he countered.

"No, really," she said. "You could have shot him and finished this whole thing right then and there."

"If I had shot him then and there we never would find out what sort of bastards he's hired to complete his task," Dancer said. "And we never find out who's hired him to destroy Project Luna.

"As it stands," Dancer said, " we now know it's Dane. I know how he thinks and how he operates. We stand a better chance than ever of seeing this project through to fruition, shutting him down, and protecting Veronique."

Jarrell arched an eyebrow. "Protecting Veronique?" she said with a hint of a smile.

"Of course," he said. "She's one of the most brilliant engineers alive and the heart of Project Luna. Of course we protect her."

Now Jarrell began to smile in earnest. "I think you want to protect her for other reasons, Philip."

It took a moment for this to sink in.

"That would be unprofessional of me," he said. "To even think of having some sort of relationship with someone I'm protecting..."

"That's not what I've heard about you, Philip," she said, now unable to conceal her enjoyment at aggravating Dancer.

He was indignant. "I have never crossed that line during a mission," he said.

"But then there's after, right?" she asked.

He shrugged. "After's different," he said.

She prepared another barb but he put his hand up. "Not now," he said. "I've cabled Bryant. Now we need to inform Veronique - I mean, Mrs. Vatine about our progress."

Jarrell could not hide her smirk as they left the hotel.

"Besides," he said. "I have an idea about how to frustrate our enemies."

"I will not shut down Project Luna!" Veronique cried in anger.

She stomped away from Dancer and Jarrell, heading towards the kitchen of her rooftop dwelling. "After all that has been done and all that has been lost in the name of progress, how could you even suggest such a thing?" she said.

Dancer shook his head. "That's not exactly what I mean," he said. "I mean to create the appearance of it being shut down."

Dancer looked up as she emerged from the kitchen. She held a mug in one hand, poised as if to throw it. Their eyes locked and she placed the mug on a nearby bookshelf. "Go on," she said.

Jarrell hid her smile behind her hand.

"Dane knows your company is headquartered here," Dancer went on. "He has attacked your facilities here, murdered your people, destroyed your resources."

"Thank you for reminding me," she said.

"But you have other facilities, don't you?" Dancer said.

"Of course," she said. "San Francisco would make a poor launch point. The actual facility is in the desert a few hours north of here by train or airship."

"But he hasn't attacked them, has he?" Dancer said.

Veronique was startled at the thought. "No. No, he hasn't," she said.

"Maybe he knows they exist, maybe he doesn't," Dancer said. "But do this: shut down everything in San Francisco. Make a show of it. Appear defeated. Then leave, and make every attempt to finish the project from your launch facility."

Veronique considered this. "If he doesn't believe we are done," she said, "he will follow us. And in so doing will discover our secret."

"There are always possibilities, of all sorts," Dancer said. "He may believe you are actually finished and call off his dogs. He may not believe and still be frustrated by your absence. He may not believe and find out where you are going.

"If he does find you," Dancer said, "Ms. Jarrell and I will still be there to protect you."

"Don't you mean protect the project?" Veronique asked, her voice and manner suddenly softer.

Dancer ignored her and kept talking. "I think this is our best move to assure your project launches on time..."

Veronique moved closer to him. "I asked you a question, Philip," she said.

She stepped closer to him. He stepped closer to her.

"Yes," he said. "The project. Of course, I meant protect the project."

A moment passed. Jarrell thought she saw sadness in Veronique's eyes.

"Very well," she said. "I will have my people shut down operations immediately. I will pack and prepare to depart first thing in the morning."

Dancer nodded. "Very well," he said. "We will prepare to join you."

Veronique left the room. Jarrell saw Dancer's shoulders slump, just a little.

"Philip," she began. He cut her off.

"Back to our rooms," he said. "We have to prepare for tomorrow."

He headed towards the elevator without looking at her. Jarrell followed without a word.

CHAPTER TWELVE

With the windows open and the train moving at speed, the heat of the desert found its way into Dancer's very bones. He despised the desert. He hated the relentless sun and the way even the wind brought no relief from the heat.

He stood in the compartment, looking at the seemingly endless wastes go by. Had the trip not been necessary he would have happily been elsewhere, perhaps by the ocean, holding the hand of a beautiful woman…

And suddenly there she was, in his mind's eye: Veronique. He was startled to find her there. But then there were her eyes. Those dazzling blue eyes.

It's always the eyes with you, he thought to himself.

She was intelligent, warm, with a wild force of will. Veronique had faced horrendous tragedy and come back stronger and smarter and better, reaching for more in a lifetime than most people would even dare to dream.

He looked from the window. Jarrell sat at a small table, reviewing files on the launch site they were rapidly approaching, preparing herself for the mission to come, as he knew he should be doing.

Jarrell. He could imagine the withering stare he would receive from her if she knew what he was thinking.

But the quick smile, the tousled blonde hair, those eyes again…

No, Philip, he thought. *The mission. Only the mission matters.*

Veronique curled up like a cat on the bed in her compartment. On the sheets in front of her were diagrams, fuel formulas, supply lists, and easily a dozen other items, each requiring immediate action, each demanding her attention.

But she found her attention wandering.

She found herself thinking of green eyes, the green eyes of a certain agent assigned to her protection, and the intensity, the danger, the excitement she saw there.

He was haunted. No, that wasn't it; Dancer was damaged. He could be cold and brutal in his work in ways that scared her, in ways her poor lost Jacques could never have been. Jacques was a dreamer, a man of vision, not always practical but sweet and kind and capable of inspiring any and everyone he had ever met, Veronique most of all.

But Dancer…

Philip…

She was sure Jacques would have laid down his life for her, though he had never been called to do so. But Dancer was here, ready to die for her, now, today, if need be.

Don't be foolish, she thought. *He's on a mission. That's what he cares about.*

But then there was that moment in her rooms back in San Francisco. Was it a slip of the tongue? Or for a moment did he betray his feelings?

What might such a man be like, one of such ability and intelligence and dedication, as a friend, a partner…a lover?

She suppressed a shiver and caught her breath. She allowed herself a smile. Perhaps there would be a moment to explore the possibilities…

But first, the mission.

Jarrell had been staring at the files on Luna Base for what seemed like days, when it had in fact been only an interminable number of hours.

She rubbed her eyes. She thought she had the layout committed more or less to memory. She had been familiar with the project for some time, but there were still some technical issues she wanted further clarification on before their arrival.

Jarrell desperately wanted coffee.

She looked across the compartment at Philip. He was staring out the window again.

She was frustrated. He really needed to be reviewing information along with her for whatever trials may lie ahead. She could feel herself getting angry, and was preparing to speak her mind.

Then she simply took a deep breath. Feelings happened. It couldn't always be helped. She trusted Dancer to do his job.

She stood from the table, sore muscles protesting. "I require coffee," she said. "How about you?"

He turned to face her. He gave a small smile. "That sounds wonderful," he said. "Cream, two sugars. And thank you."

She nodded curtly and exited the compartment. She made her way down the train's corridor towards the dining car, following the smells of something delicious. She dodged various passengers on the way, most of them focused on papers or documents of some kind, too busy to notice another human in the hallway.

She entered the dining car, spotting a waiter and preparing her request when she heard something.

It sounded like a gunshot.

Then she heard the sound of horses' hooves pounding on the hard-packed ground outside the train.

Her pulse began to race. Jarrell rushed to a window and found her fears confirmed.

A band of gunmen pursued the train.

One of them took aim with a rifle of a type Jarrell had never seen before. He fired, and it tore a hole in the side of the train big enough to ride a horse through.

CHAPTER THIRTEEN

The sound of gunfire snapped Dancer out of his reverie and back to the all-too-real.

He left the compartment at a dead run, entering the corridor and dodging other passengers as they ran from the action.

Dancer ran toward it.

He arrived at the dining car and found Jarrell crouching behind a pile of debris as cover. He joined her. She glanced at him, all the acknowledgement she could spare.

Dancer looked out the side of the train car. There was ample room where the attackers' fire had destroyed a large part of the wall. He saw their attackers – a band of four on horseback, wearing dark leather, firing guns at the train.

Dancer spotted the rider he assumed was the leader. The man wielded a heavy rifle.

Dancer's blood ran cold. He recognized the rifle.

"They're from Conner," he said.

"How do you know?" Jarrell asked.

"That heavy rifle," Dancer said. "He didn't have a name for it – but it's from Goff's shop."

The rider came closer to the train. He raised the rifle.

There was no time to think.

Jarrell rose from cover, charged across the debris of the dining car to the hole, and leapt into the air.

She had taken action so quickly that Dancer hadn't even the time to wish her luck.

Jarrell locked eyes with the leader as she hurtled through the air at him.

He was stunned, to say the least. His eyes were wide with an emotion Jarrell couldn't place – fear? Surprise?

It didn't matter. She had timed her jump more perfectly than she'd hoped. Her boots caught the rider in the face, and he fell from the saddle, arms waving, rifle in the air.

With one hand, Jarrell gripped the pommel of the saddle. She swung herself around onto the horse, and with her other hand grabbed the rifle out of the air a split second before it would have been out of reach.

Dancer watched the scant seconds this took. "Damn," he said. "How did she do that in a dress?"

The lead rider fell under the hooves of his own horse. He screamed briefly before falling forever silent.

Jarrell knew she had only a heartbeat before the other riders targeted her. She had the only one of the heavy rifles. She examined it quickly – how many shots did it have left? She had no way to know.

She tugged the reins, steering the horse away from the train, splitting the attention of the three remaining attackers

Dancer took aim with his pistol. Regular bullets pinged off surfaces around him. He ignored them, carefully taking aim, slowly pulling the trigger.

One of Goff's special bullets hit its mark.

A spray of liquid ceramic erupted from the impact point, instantly hardening over the arm and hand of the attacker. Alarmed and with his range of motion compromised, the man panicked, falling from his horse and hitting the ground with an audible crack.

He was still.

Two riders had Jarrell in their sights.

Bullets sizzled past her.

She felt a hot slash on her right thigh. She gasped from the pain but kept her focus and kept riding.

She raised the rifle and took aim at one of the riders.

She pulled the trigger.

The rifle's recoil was monstrous but again she stayed on her horse.

The roar of the weapon deafened her. She therefore had no idea if the man she'd shot with it made a sound before the impact of the shot blasted him to bloody chunks.

His horse fell to the ground, rolling from the impact of the weapon. Blood sprayed from the animal's back, and its legs crumpled. Jarrell felt a stab of pain in her heart at the sight, she'd never have hurt the animal on purpose, but it was too late to take the shot back.

Jarrell spun and aimed at the last rider. She aimed and pulled the trigger.

The rifle only clicked. Jarrell swore under her breath. She was out of ammunition.

But the last rider didn't know that.

Jarrell kept the rifle pointed at the last rider a second longer. No doubt fearing a painful death at the hands of the weapon, he turned his horse and rode in the other direction.

Jarrell rode back towards the train. It had not slowed down. Dancer stood at the damaged wall and held his hand towards her. She reached her hand to his, taking it, feeling his strong grip as he pulled her off the horse and back into the train.

They collapsed on the floor of the wrecked dining car, panting for breath.

"You're bleeding," he said.

"I'll bandage it," she said.

"That was quite a wonder to watch," he said.

She smiled at the compliment. "Thank you," she said.

They looked up at the sound of a footstep. Veronique stood there, looking at them, anger in her eyes.

"I think we might say, Philip," she said, "that your plan was ill advised."

Dancer glanced at Jarrell before facing Veronique. "I'm sorry," he said.

"I just pray your foolishness doesn't bring down the entire project," she said, her eyes blazing, before walking away.

CHAPTER FOURTEEN

The crimson of the setting sun illuminated the train as it pulled into the small station with a hiss of steam and a squeal of metal. Dancer stepped off the train onto the weathered wooden platform, Jarrell following close behind with only a barely noticeable limp.

The station was about one hundred yards from the lip of a broad canyon. A hard dirt path, with only a rough handrail, marked the way.

Others disembarked the train – engineers, technicians, support staff – and made their way down the path. Dancer and Jarrell joined them.

"You haven't told me a great deal about Luna Base," Dancer began.

Jarrell smiled. "I have no particular way with words," she said. "I would not have been able to do it justice."

Dancer cocked an eyebrow. "Really, now," he said. "How hard could it be to describe a great flock of eggheads in the desert?"

Jarrell's smile did not waver as they approached the edge of the canyon, or as Dancer looked over it.

His jaw dropped.

The canyon was deep, and wide, and full nearly to the edge with buzzing activity. There were more buildings than he could easily count, some of wood, some of brick, some of polished metal. He could see electricity crackle from some, unknown gasses rising from others, loud sounds of machines whirring away. Cables and walkways extended from wall to wall and floor to edge, like a web spun by a deranged spider. Scientists and technicians of every description rushed along every available surface attending to tasks Dancer could scarcely imagine.

But this was the least of what Dancer saw.

"You know," he said, "I don't think I actually believed you. I didn't think you were lying, exactly... I just didn't think it could actually be real."

Jarrell nodded. "I know exactly how you feel."

Before them, at the center of the mad web of science before them, stood a gantry of steel and brass. And within that gantry stood the great ship herself.

"Behold," Jarrell said softly, "Artemis."

She was a six-story tower of steel and brass, covered with vents and hatches and panels, hooked up to dozens of cables. A dome of glass stood atop her, and workmen of every kind occupied the gantry, performing tasks and duties that beggared description.

Dancer loved her on site. "The moon, you say?" he said quietly. Jarrell nodded. "I believe it," he said.

Before he could say anything further, Veronique walked past them without a word. Even in the heat of the desert day he felt a shiver as she passed by.

"It's a miracle none of her people were hurt during the attack," Jarrell said.

"I know," Dancer said. "Death is a part of our business. I accept that it could come for me at any moment. I've spent my career trying to delay - or sometimes hasten - its arrival for others. She's angry at me, that my decision endangered her people."

He bowed his head. "She's not remotely as angry as I am."

Veronique descended the stairs to ground level in the canyon. Luna base buzzed around her. She took pleasure in the activity, the purposeful direction of energy towards a grand goal.

The moment did not last.

Dancer had misjudged, badly. She was not given to fear, certainly not for herself, but its cold claws reached around her heart in a way she despised. Years of imagination and effort, of mistakes made and rectified, of vision – all at risk because that man convinced her to take a risk.

She had to put it out of her mind. She had to be keen of mind in these next hours if something was to be salvaged from the situation she found herself in.

Two men approached her, the crowd of workers parting before them as they made their way to her. One was tall, slender, bookish, but with a core of steel that became evident the more you knew him: Wells. The other was just as tall, but broad, with a gleaming bald head and a bushy red beard: Verne. Wells was from the U.S. Army, an invaluable ally. Verne had been one of closest friends in America ever since her arrival on her shores.

Wells reached out his hand. She took it, shook it, offered him a smile. Verne embraced her in his bearish arms. He stepped back and looked her in the eye. "Veronique," he began, "how did they know? How could they have followed you?"

"A spy," Wells said, "someone in our organization."

"It doesn't matter," she said. "We have to move. Now."

Wells shook his head, anxiety written across his features. "We can't," he said. "The schedule is too accelerated, we risk compromising the whole project."

Veronique looked him in the eye. "We have no choice," she said. "We risk discovery and destruction otherwise.

"Artemis launches in twelve hours."

CHAPTER FIFTEEN

The chamber was hewn from the rock wall of the canyon. It was cool and quiet, a stark contrast to the rest of Luna Base.

Jarrell sat in a superbly overstuffed and comfortable easy chair, a pot of hot coffee on the small round table next to her. She had added cream and an unreasonable amount of sugar, and it tasted wonderful as it went down.

Verne and Wells occupied their own chairs, drinking their own coffee, some of which might have had additions of bourbon. They had a look of exhaustion about them, like she imagined she must have.

"Thank you for taking a few moments to see me, my friends," Jarell said. "I know the work still ahead of you, the pressure you must feel right now."

"We have a moment to spare for you, my dear Madeline. It's so good to see you, old friend," said Verne. "After such danger on the journey here!"

Jarrell shrugged. "All part of the job," she said. "And it's good to the two of you, as well. I'm at best only tangential to this project, but I am so proud to see what you've accomplished! It's exciting to think we're only hours away from sending mankind into space."

"Indeed," Verne said. "I know Wells here is angry about accelerating the time table, but I think – I think we're ready. I think it's time."

"So," Wells began, changing the subject, "this man Dane wants to destroy Project Luna."

Jarrell swallowed a sip of coffee. "It's not what he wants," she said. "We think he's been hired to do so. But he's the one behind the attacks on your San Francisco facilities, and we believe he's most likely on his way here, now."

Wells and Verne traded a worried look. "Did you lead Dane here?" Wells asked.

Jarrell was silent for a moment. "Yes," she said. "I believe we did."

"After all these years, all the effort expended, you and your friend Dancer put this all at risk!" Wells exploded.

Verne looked at Wells, shocked at the outburst. "My good man!" Verne shouted.

Jarrell gestured for Verne to be silent. She looked at Wells. "We made a decision. We made it in an attempt to preserve this project and to preserve lives," she said quietly, and then, in nearly a whisper, "We were wrong."

Wells glared at her for long seconds. Then he seemed almost to deflate. "I apologize," he said. "I never anticipated a sustained campaign against our work. I should blame neither you nor Mr. Dancer for your best efforts."

Jarrell smiled, reached out to take each of their hands. "We are far from finished, my friends," she said. "Verne, finish your work. Prepare Artemis. The ship *will* launch."

She turned to Wells. "Marshall your forces. Summon your troops. We have a defense to prepare."

CHAPTER SIXTEEN

The room was long and low, its walls and ceilings gleaming steel, its air artificially cool, brisk, and dry. Unusually clear and white electric light made the chamber almost seem to glow.

Dancer and Jarrell had entered behind Veronique. Various technicians orbited around two people at the far end of the room. As they grew closer to them, Dancer saw a man and a woman, each being outfitted in what looked live dive suits, but sleeker.

Technicians parted, making way for Veronique. She gestured at the two in the dive suits. "Please meet Michael Alberto and Barbara Binder," she said. "They are the two people we have selected as the crew for Artemis."

Dancer and Jarrell each reached out their hands, taking those of Alberto and Binder and shaking them firmly. "It's a pleasure to meet you," Dancer said.

"I'm familiar with the project," Jarrell said, "I've read both your files. There could not be two more suited for the challenge before them."

Alberto smiled. He had jet dark hair, oiled back and gleaming, and a rascal's smile. "I'm glad you think so," he said. "All I can think of at this moment are the things I don't know."

"Nonsense," Veronique said. "You have multiple degrees, in engineering and geology, are an experienced airship pilot, and are in peek physical condition."

Jarrell nodded. Dancer thought he caught her eyebrow rising as Veronique mentioned "peeks physical condition," but let it go. Instead he cocked his eyebrow and asked, "And you, Ms. Binder? Are you in peek condition as well?"

Dancer felt a short shock of pain to one of his shins as someone kicked him. He glanced at Veronique and saw blooms of red on her cheeks.

"I have extensive medical training," Binder said. "My father was a battlefield medic in the war, and he taught me much of what to do – and what not to do – in an emergency. I've also studied with excellent physicians in Europe."

She smirked. "It's my job to keep us alive until we get back," she said.

"How do you know what kinds of problems you'll face?" Jarrell asked.

"Some we can anticipate, like the difficulties of dealing with vacuum," Binder said. "As to how many others and what they might be…" she trailed off. "We'll just have to see."

"We should go," Veronique said. "They are in their final preparations and need to continue."

Goodbyes were said. Veronique led the two agents from the chamber, through corridors and back into the bustle of the base. Cool air wrapped around them.

"I wanted you to meet them," she said. "To understand something of the human lives at the center of all this.

Dancer looked up. The night sky was clear, each star a pinpoint of light in a sea of black ink. And then there was the moon itself, so bright and close Dancer felt he could almost touch it.

"I'm jealous, you know," he began. "I'd go myself, if I could."

"Alberto and Binder were chosen in part for their judgment under pressure," Veronique said. "I think that would rule you out, no?"

Dancer turned to look at her, a curious expression on his face. "Madeline," he said, "if you could leave us for a moment?"

Jarrell nodded curtly, without a word, and walked away.

Dancer and Veronique stood there quietly. Neither heard the commotion around them because all they noticed was each other.

Dancer looked at Veronique. "I'm sorry," he said. "I'm in a hard business. I'm only human. Mistakes get made. Accidents happen. People die."

She looked back. Her blue eyes carried the weight of pain and loss.

"I trusted you," she said. "With my company, the lives of my people, the fate of my dream."

Dancer began to speak. She placed a finger against his lips.

"After my husband died, I thought I might never feel again. Then I had a new dream, a dream of the sky and the stars. And it was good and I was happy. But there was something missing and I didn't even know what it was until I met you."

She then reached up, grabbed Dancer by the back of his head, and drew him down to her, kissing him with a hunger that truth be told scared them both.

"But I cannot trust you right now," she said. "Not until you prove yourself to me. Not until Artemis is away."

She let go of him, turned, and walked away.

CHAPTER SEVENTEEN

The airship soared through the night sky. Its skin, painted black, made it all but invisible to anyone who might be observing from the ground.

Connor Dane stood on her flight deck, observing the crew. They were making good time. The exact location of his destination was unknown to him, but he felt certain he would know it when he saw it.

After all, a base devoted to sending men to the moon would have to be fairly conspicuous.

He looked out the windows of the flight deck. All her saw was desert and clouds and stars, and all wrapped in the night. He turned wordlessly from the view, exited the flight deck, and walked back into the airship.

He found the passenger cabins. The doors of each cabin were open, spilling into a common area, where his men were busy making preparations. They each wore dark military style clothing and were inspecting, cleaning, and preparing a wide variety of weapons for the coming attack.

Dane nodded his approval, telling the mercenaries to carry on, and returned to the flight deck.

He continued his vigil, observing the darkness for signs of light and life.

What the hell was he doing?

It was one thing to take money to wreak havoc and death on people who had it coming anyway. But Vatine and her people were trying to expand the breadth of human knowledge, to build a pathway to a grander frontier than anyone had ever explored.

Had he fallen so far? And for what - money, or what it could buy?

What could he do?

He could simply leave, and take the way out he had taken with Philip all those months ago. He could order the ship turned around, declare the mission a failure. He could set a fuse, explode the ship's hydrogen, and kill the bastards he had hired while he made good an escape. No one would miss them.

But then there were the people who had hired him. They did not accept failure. And if his mission failed... They would search the world for him, just to be sure. Dane was very good at what he did, and very good at changing his face, his name, his identity. But his employers had money, and time, and a limitless capacity for vengeance.

And then there was Philip.

Sure, he had tried to kill Philip, but that was only because Philip was trying to bring him in for treason. It was nothing personal on Dane's part.

But it was damn sure going to be personal for Philip next time. And Philip Arthur Dancer had a way of resolving things he took personally.

A cry went up from one of the crew. Dane snapped from his reverie and looked out the window where the man was pointing.

A golden glow shown on the horizon. The pilot steered the airship towards in that direction. In minutes, Dane knew they had their target.

Luna Base.

He shrugged, all considerations at an end. This was his mission, his employment, and all other considerations fell away.

"Men!" he cried. "Prepare for battle!"

CHAPTER EIGHTEEN

The launch crew had assessed their accelerated timetable, and so, an hour before dawn, final preparations were being made for launch of Artemis.

The ship was bathed in light. Thick pipes and cables were connected to her, loading atmosphere, water, and fuel. A gantry connected the pilots' module to their staging area.

Dancer stood on a deck with a superb view of the whole affair. He watched as Alberto and Binder, now fully suited, crossed the gantry and entered their module.

Jarrell walked onto the deck. Wells was with her. For a moment, Dancer thought one or all three of them might cry. And then he decided he didn't care anymore, and let the tears flow.

"It's beautiful," he said. "Mr. Wells, you and your people are to be lauded in every manner possible."

Wells was having his own problems with his emotions, but after a moment, he pulled himself together. "Thank you, Mr. Dancer," Wells said.

Jarrell smiled to herself. "Maybe I'll get to go someday," she said.

"If this works," Wells said, "there may well be no limit to what we can accomplish in space."

Dancer considered this. He was about to reply - when an explosion rocked the base. A fireball spread, throwing ghastly orange light on the scene, and throwing technicians in the air.

All emotions gone save cold hate, Dancer looked up. It was difficult, but he could see the outline of an all-black airship rimed in the light of the fire.

Wells was gone without a word, no doubt to rally his troops. Sharpshooters, trained for such an attack, were already on the rim of the canyon firing upon the airship.

There was another explosion. The great Artemis herself was still unharmed. Shortly, ropes descended from the black airship, which armed attackers then used to repel down.

Dancer and Jarrell moved into action.

They raced down the deck's access ladder and to the floor of the canyon. They each had their weapons ready in less time than it takes to tell of it. The attackers were firing weapons of all kinds, in every direction, seemingly with no plan other than destruction. Technicians fell, screaming, wounded. Some fell, dead.

Dancer took aim, and fired, and fired again.

Jarrell fired as well, but her rage was even more blinding. She waded into a group of attackers, and began fighting them hand to hand. Despite the danger he was in, Dancer was truly impressed by the sight of her as she rained injury and death on the richly deserving.

After their immediate area was clear, they took a moment to catch their breath and plan.

"The launch must be protected," Jarrell said.

"No arguments," Dancer said. "And at any cost. We make our way to the control room, yes?"

"No," Jarrell said. "If Artemis has to it can launch without aid from the control room."

"But the control room – " Dancer began.

"Veronique is in the control room," Jarrell said, "I know. But she'd tell you the ship comes first, Mr. Dancer."

Dancer looked at his partner. He hated it, but he knew she was right.

"To the gantry, then," he said.

Jarrell nodded once. As she turned to go Jarrell thought he saw her smile, and in the orange light of the fire, he found her frightening indeed.

The pair made their way through the fighting. Wells had indeed rallied his troops, and between them and the sharpshooters on the canyon rim, fast work was being made of the attackers.

Dancer saw two, however, that were making their way expertly to the gantry. He gestured to Jarrell and they quickly followed. They arrived at the foundation of the gantry, looked up, and saw the attackers scaling the metal framework. Dancer and Jarrell each grabbed a handhold and began scaling it in pursuit, each picking a target.

Jarrell reached hers first. The noise of the battle masked the sounds of their pursuit, and Jarrell reached out, grabbed the man's boot, and pulled with all her might. Taken by surprise, the man lost his grip and plummeted to the canyon floor, bouncing off the gantry on the way. He lay still.

Dancer's target was not taken unaware. He pulled a revolver from a holster and took aim at Dancer. Dancer waited until the last possible instant before the man pulled the trigger to swing inside the gantry.

The sound of the revolver was loud and the bullet was hot as it creased his back, but Dancer was alive. The attacker would either keep going or come back for the kill. Dancer took the split second he had, pulled the revolver he kept loaded with Goff's bullets, and looked behind him.

The attacker appeared.

Dancer fired, striking his target in the chest.

The man screamed as acid from Goff's round ate away at his chest. He fell, dead before he hit the ground.

Jarrell came to Dancer. She looked over the wound on his back. "We have to get you to a doctor," she said.

"Not yet," he said. "We have one more task. We have to take the airship."

Dancer quickly descended the gantry, with Jarrell close behind.

CHAPTER NINETEEN

They had moments, no more, to figure out how to board the attacking airship.

And then Dancer saw their answer.

The ropes the attackers had used to descend from the airship were still hanging!

Behind them, they heard a great burst of ferocious energy from the Artemis and a cacophonous blast of mechanical noise. The air seemed to warm up around them and the hairs on their arms stood on end.

Dancer and Jarrell traded a look. "Come on!" Dancer said. "Follow me!"

The airship was moving into position to attack the Artemis. Dancer grabbed one rope and Jarrell another and they began to climb as quickly as they could. Below them they heard the sounds of great clamps disengaging. Though Dancer and Jarrell could not see it from their precarious climb, a hatch slid wide on the underside of the

Artemis and suddenly the gantry and indeed the entire base were bathed in the glow of the harnessed Wellsite. The directed energy of the exotic mineral began to lift the Artemis, slowly at first, then with more speed as it cleared the gantry and made for the sky and the stars beyond.

The airship rose as Dancer climbed the rope. His injury nearly made him cry out in pain but he'd be damned if he let it stop him. He made the mistake of looking down and saw the base receding ever more quickly below him.

He looked up and saw open bay doors in the belly of the airship. He was growing ever closer. Just a few more feet, just a little more effort and he would be there. When he thought his reserves were exhausted, when he could feel his arms weakening, when he was afraid he would fall to his doom, a hand reached down to grab his arm.

Jarrell!

She had reached the bay just moments ahead of him, and just moments before he would have fallen. With a grunt of effort, she hauled him into the bay, where they lay exhausted on the deck.

But they had no time for exhaustion.

They picked themselves up and examined their surroundings. The bay was most likely used for cargo; in this case the cargo had been death for hire. The wind howled in the bay, making conversation difficult, but by now it was hardly needed. Dancer gestured towards the front of the airship. Jarrell knew to follow. They headed forward, silent as they did so, careful of who or what they might find.

They found an empty ship. Most or all of the crew must have offloaded to attack Luna Base. They found empty passageways and quiet chambers.

They came to the hatch that led to the flight deck. Not even a glance was needed as each drew a weapon while striding forward. Dancer knocked the hatch open with a single kick fueled by rage. They entered the flight deck and found Connor Dane behind the controls of the ship.

Dancer looked at Dane. "You rotten no good son of a bitch," Dancer said.

"You have much to answer for," Jarrell said.

Dane let go the controls, his back to Dancer and Jarrell. He removed a small pistol from his belt and before he could be stopped he fired several shots into the controls, wrecking them.

"You fool!" Dancer shouted. "What have you done?"

"Doomed this ship, I hope," Dane said. "And you with it."

"Your mission has failed," Jarrell said. "You'll never catch the Artemis now. She's well on her way."

Dane nodded. "But I'll have the satisfaction of your ends, my dear."

No more needed to be said. Jarrell moved in on one side, Dancer on the other. Dane struck first, feinting at Jarrell before sending a devastating blow at Dancer's jaw. Dancer dodged but felt the breath of the wind as Dane's fist sped past his head.

Jarrell moved in, pointing the muzzle of her pistol at Dane's head. He moved, blindingly fast, as her finger squeezed the trigger. The shots tore through the flight deck's windows, shattering glass and inviting the roar of the wind.

Every lose object in the room instantly became airborne. Dane swung his hand at a map that plastered itself to his face and when he regained his sight Dancer had his gun pointed at Dane's guts.

Dancer smiled as he fired.

The round tore into Dane's guts and he fell to the deck.

Dancer moved close to his former friend. Dane coughed blood.

"So," he said, "a little gift from our friend Mr. Goff?"

"You'll find out soon," Dancer replied.

He then noticed something under Dane's coat.

"I can't believe it," Dancer shouted over the wind. "It's the wingpak!"

"What?" Jarrell said.

"The wingpak! The gliding device Goff tried to sell me! It was how Dane survived out last match! Here, help me," Dancer said. Together he and Jarrell removed it from Dane, who was not quite dead yet but too weak to argue.

"What's your plan?" she asked Dancer.

"We're going to escape with this," he said, strapping it on. Jarrell went pale and looked as if she was about to say something.

"No time to argue!" he shouted as he grabbed her and leapt through the broken windows.

Jarrell screamed as they fell through the dawn sky toward the floor of the desert far below. Dancer pulled a cord on the contraption and great gliding wings sprung from it, slowing their descent.

Above them, the airship exploded. Great orange tongues of flame spread across the sky and the remains of the black craft began a swift descent to the desert.

Dancer struggled with the wingpak. Their descent was slowing, but not enough.

There! A river cutting through the dry land!

Dancer angled his flight. His exhausted muscles struggled with the device. The desert floor was coming up terrifying fast.

And then there was cool running water as they hit the river.

They went under. The wings were wrecked by the landing, wrapping themselves around Dancer. Jarrell, disoriented by the landing, forced herself to focus on Dancer. He was thrashing around in the water, desperate, bubbles escaping his lips, the last of his air lost.

Jarrell found a release on the device and pulled it. The wingpak dropped away in the current, flowing away. She grabbed Dancer by the collar and hauled him to the shore.

They lay there for some time, exhausted, breathing in the cool morning air and letting the rays of the sun dry them. A while later, neither knew how long, Jarrell finally spoke. "Not that I'm complaining, mind you," she said. "But why did the airship explode?"

"The last round I fired from the collection I purchased from Herr Goff," Dancer said. "It was a timed explosive."

Jarrell sat up and looked at Dancer. "You fired a bomb…into Dane's guts?" she asked.

Dancer nodded. "Yes, I did. You see, this time I wanted to be sure."

CHAPTER TWENTY

Eventually, rescuers came. Dancer and Jarrell were gingerly loaded onto wagons and brought to Luna Base. They were tended to by the base's medical stuff and cleared for travel. They then boarded a train back to San Francisco, where they were taken by Veronique's people to an exceedingly comfortable house on a bluff overlooking San Francisco Bay.

After a week's convalescence, Dancer still could not wipe the smile off his face. Jarrell was beginning to find it insufferable, but she kept her peace about it. Ushering your most grievous enemy to an ignominious end had a way of putting a person in a good humor, she thought.

On a foggy, cool morning of their second week in the house, one in which no comfort had been denied, Dancer was walking the veranda, drinking hot sweet coffee, looking at the gray waters of the bay, when Veronique pulled up in a carriage.

Dancer watched her approach the house. She wore a simple blue dress that brought out the vividness of her eyes, even in the fog. She stepped up on the veranda, only then noticing that he was outside observing her.

They stood for a long moment, neither saying a word, but only looking in each other's eyes.

"Good morning, Veronique," Philip said. "You're looking well this morning."

"Good morning to you as well, Philip," she replied. "You look well too, all things considered."

"Well," he said, "if my recuperative powers were not substantial I should already have been a dead man several times over."

"I'm glad you are well," she said. She took a step closer to him. "I was...unkind, Philip. And wondering if you might...forgive me."

He raised a hand to her face. He cupped it gently. She placed her hand on his and closed her eyes and smiled.

"I was never angry at you," he said. "You had every right to be angry with me. So for my part, there is nothing to forgive."

They withdrew their hands. Veronique opened her eyes. "I am curious," she said with a devilish little smile, "how well you are actually feeling."

Dancer returned her smile. "Let's go find out."

Dancer entered the house and Veronique followed. They walked upstairs to Dancer's room, entered, and quietly closed the door.

That afternoon, Dancer and Veronique decided to take lunch on the veranda. They were hungry, and ate heartily, of fresh fish, fruit, bread warm from the oven, and a delicious white wine. Later, the household staff alleged that laughter was heard.

"Contact was established with Artemis," Veronique said. "They were unable to complete their intended journey to the moon, sadly. Apparently there are mathematics necessary yet to be worked out. They orbited the earth for perhaps 36 hours before directing their ship to return to earth. They landed – even more roughly than you and your associate – in the ocean not far from here."

"What happened?" Dancer asked.

"Alberto and Binder escaped with their lives," she said. "And we were able to recover the ship herself. Thankfully, though the seas were rough, the ship proved resistant to sinking."

"Are you disappointed?" Dancer asked.

Veronique looked startled. "Disappointed? Philip, we have placed human beings in orbit around the earth! We have made possible a new age of men!" she said.

"Forgive me," he said. "I am not a man of vision, in the end. I suppose I take my life and my work a day at a time."

They were quiet for a moment, enjoying the breeze and the smell of the ocean.

"What shall we do, Philip?" Veronique asked.

"It seems we are each tied to our work," he said. "Would you leave your work to accompany me?"

She looked at him sadly, and shook her head.

"And I'm afraid my work is too large a part of who I am to leave it for you," he said.

"So here we are," she said.

"But my work takes me everywhere," he continued. "Including here. And life is both too long and too short to ever really say goodbye."

He rose from his chair and took her hand. "So what do you say we make the most of today while we have it?"

She smiled. He reached down, lifted her from her chair, took her in his arms, and marched back into the house.

A week later Philip Dancer was on a train heading east, accompanied by the redoubtable Madeline Jarrell. As it happens, they had each had enough of airship travel for a while.

He sat in their compartment, looking out the window at the land speeding by. Jarrell was reading a book. They enjoyed the companionable silence. Soon, the train reached a station, and with a hiss of steam and a grind of metal, they came to a halt.

They each heard footsteps pounding down the corridor outside before the door opened. A porter appeared, waving a telegram.

"Are you Mr. Dancer and Ms. Jarrell?" he asked, panting, out of breath. They nodded yes. "Incredible! This cable arrived for you just minutes before your train did!"

Dancer took the cable from the porter's hand. His eyes buzzed over it before rolling back.

Jarrell smiled ruefully. "Let me guess," she said. "Bryant."

"Bryant," Dancer said. "How he found us here, I don't know."

"Let me guess again: is there perhaps a job for us?" Jarrell asked.

"Ms. Jarrell," he said, "However did you know?"